Busy-Busy Bears

story by
Hiawyn Oram
with pictures by Frédéric Joos

Andersen Press
London

Baby Bear was dressing Bella Doll.
"Uh . . . which dress? Which dress?"
"The blue," said Big Bear.
"The pink!" said Baby Bear.

With Bella Doll in pink, Baby Bear sat down to breakfast.
"Hmm . . . which cereal? Which cereal?"
"Hot oats," said Big Bear.
"Happy Nutty Crunchies!" said Baby Bear.
"Fine," said Big Bear. "Now you help me with something.
Mr Baker Bear has offered me a job. Shall I say yes or . . . ?"

Baby Bear dropped her spoon in her cereal.
"A JOB?" she cried. "Like the one Baby Tiger's mummy goes to all the time?"

Big Bear took Baby Bear onto her lap.
"It'll only be one day a week," she explained. "Just one day, that's all!"
"But what'll happen to ME?" cried Baby Bear.
"You'll be safe and sound with Mrs Hogg," said Big Bear.

So next day, Big Bear put on her new baker-shop apron and took Baby Bear and a big bag of toys and books round to Mrs Hogg's.

But as soon as
Baby Bear took
out a toy . . .

. . . Mrs Hogg put it back to keep things tidy.

And when Baby Bear
took out her favourite book,
Mrs Hogg fell asleep after
she'd only read two pages.

And when Mrs Hogg woke up and Baby Bear showed her
how she could do headstands on a cushion, Mrs Hogg didn't say,
"Very good!" or "Show me another one!" She just said, "Hmmm,"
and knitted and knitted and KNITTED . . .

. . . until Baby Bear was so tired
of watching she went to sit on the step
and wait for Big Bear.

"And here I am!"
cried Big Bear, sweeping
Baby Bear into her arms.

"Did you have a good day?" Big Bear asked,
as they walked the best way home .
    "No," said Baby Bear. "Because I missed you."
    "And I missed you, too," said Big Bear, "when I wasn't
very busy."

"Well, I missed you ALL the time!" said Baby Bear
as they got home and began to make their supper.
"Every, every, single, single moment I missed you!"
"Hmmm," said Big Bear, "we can't have that!
So I'd better tell Mr Baker Bear I can't do the job."

"Good," said Baby Bear putting Bella Doll to bed
on the sofa. "Unless . . ." She peered over the sofa arm.
"Unless . . . when you go off to work, I go off to the
playgroup Baby Tiger goes to . . ."

So that's what Big Bear arranged, and the next time she went off to work, Baby Bear went to Baby Tiger's playgroup.

She played with Baby Tiger
in the playgroup garden,

and the playgroup sandpit,

and the playgroup tent.

She did two enormous paintings at the painting table . . .

and made a messy model at the modelling table.

She built half a castle with Baby Tiger while Baby Fox
and Baby Weasel built the other half.

She slid and slid and SLID down the slippy slide . . .

and helped settle an argument about who had
had the most turns on the tyre swing.

She played the xylophone,

the castanets,

and the drums . . .

and had a giant game of fishing with Baby Fox and Baby Mole.
And just as she'd nearly worked out how the magnets worked . . .

suddenly there was Big Bear come to pick her up
and take her home!

"Well . . . ?" said Big Bear. "How was your day?"
"Busy!" cried Baby Bear. "Busy! Busy! Busy! So busy-busy,
I didn't even have time to miss you once!"

"Good!" laughed Big Bear taking off her baker's apron . . .

"Good, good, GOOD!" she said, putting her feet up with a cup of tea and a soft sigh. "Because now Mr Baker Bear has asked if I'll work THREE days a week!"

"Then tell him YES, of course!" said Baby Bear, jumping up beside Big Bear. "Tell him Yes! Yes! Yes! And do you know why?"

"Why?" said Big Bear . . .

"Because," said Baby Bear,
"when YOU go off to YOUR work,
I'LL be off to MY work . . .

PLAYING HARD ALL DAY!"